Ghost Striker

J. BURCHETT AND S. VOGLER

Illustrated by Guy Parker-Rees

BLOOMSBURY

LONDON BERLIN NEW YORK

For our friends Lorraine and Lee Middleburgh
with love

Bloomsbury Publishing, London, Berlin and New York

First published in Great Britain in 1999 by Bloomsbury Publishing Plc
36 Soho Square, London, W1D 3QY
This edition published in July 2010

Text copyright © Janet Burchett and Sara Vogler 1999
Illustrations copyright © Guy Parker-Rees 1999
The moral rights of the author and illustrator have been asserted

A CIP catalogue record of this book is available from the British Library

ISBN 978 1 4088 0828 3

FSC
Mixed Sources
Product group from well-managed
forests and other controlled sources
Cert no. SGS-COC-2061
www.fsc.org
© 1996 Forest Stewardship Council

Printed in Great Britain by Clays Ltd, St Ives plc, Bungay, Suffolk

1 3 5 7 9 10 8 6 4 2

www.bloomsbury.com/childrens

Ghost Striker

It was a big day for the Tigers
Under-Tens Football Team.
They were going to play the
Galleywood Gazelles in the
final of the Junior County
Championship. If the Tigers

won, they would take the County Shield home to Tottingham Town.

It was ten minutes before the big match. The Tigers ran on to the pitch. All except their striker, Billy Bright. Billy walked slowly out of the changing room. He looked worried.

'What's up, Billy?' asked Rob.

'It's Dad,' said Billy. 'He's got a problem.'

Billy's dad was the Tigers' coach.

'What's the matter with him?' said Blocker. 'He was all right just now.'

'Things always happen to Mr Bright,' moaned Joe.

'Perhaps he's tripped over his bootlaces,' giggled Mona, the goalkeeper.

'Perhaps his legs have fallen off,' laughed Ellen.

'No,' sighed Billy. 'He's stuck in the toilet.'

'Is he locked in?' asked Lisa.

'We'll get him out,' said Rob.

'I'll climb over the door,' offered Bullseye.

'I wouldn't,' said Billy, shaking his head, 'he's not locked in. He's being sick.'

'Has he got a bug?' asked Terry.

'No,' sighed Billy. 'He didn't have time for lunch, so he gobbled down his birthday chocolates – all three boxes.'

'What are we going to do?' asked Blocker.

'We're hopeless without a

coach,' said Kim.

'Billy will coach us,' said
Rick. 'Won't you, Billy?'

'Yes,' said Lisa. 'We'll be all
right with Billy and his book.
We're the Tigers . . .'

Billy didn't join in. The Tigers
thought that Billy was a great
coach. They thought he had
help from a coaching book. He
couldn't tell them the truth.
Billy did have help – but it
wasn't from a book. He was
helped by the famous Springer
Spannell. Everyone had heard
of Springer. He'd been a
brilliant goalkeeper for
Tottingham Town FC. People
still talked about the time he
saved a vital penalty in the FA
Cup Final. No one else knew
that Springer helped Billy,
because no one else could see
him. Springer Spannell was . . .
a ghost! And he was only
allowed to appear to one

person. It was in his PhIFA
rules.

Billy looked up and down the
pitch. He was a useless coach

Phantoms In Football (PhiFA) Rules
RULE SEVEN : A GHOST COACH
CAN ONLY APPEAR TO ONE
MEMBER OF THE TEAM, AND
IF ANYONE ELSE FINDS OUT,
THE COACH GETS THE SACK
AND DISAPPEARS.

on his own. And there was no sign of Springer.

'Come on, Springer,' he muttered.

'Come on, Billy,' called Terry. 'Let's get going.'

'Right,' said Billy nervously. 'Erm . . . we'll loosen up.'

'Loosen up what?' asked Kim.

'Er . . .' said Billy. 'Arms . . . necks . . . knees . . . teeth!'

'Looks like they've got ants in their pants!' said a voice.

Billy looked round. A man was standing on the pitch, balancing a football on his head. He was wobbly round the edges and Billy could see right through him. It was like

looking through a gooseberry
jelly.

'Springer!' yelled Billy.

'You want us to spring?'
gasped Blocker. 'I can't jump
and wiggle my ears at the same
time.'

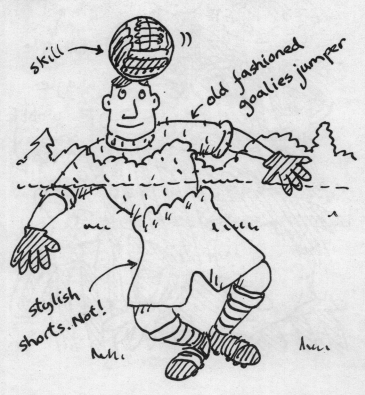

'Not you, Blocker,' sighed
Billy.

The ghost goalie stuck his
ball under his arm.

'Sorry I'm late, Billy,' he
said. 'My bike had a puncture.
Where's your dad this time?'

'Being sick in the toilet,'
muttered Billy, embarrassed.

'He had too many chocolates for lunch.'

'Oh dear,' said Springer. 'Tell him to stick to sandwiches next time. I see the team's warmed up. Let's get ready for kick-off.'

Billy ran on to the pitch. The Tigers picked themselves up and

followed him to their positions.
Springer jogged up and down
on the touchline.

'Tell Mona their little striker
is very fast,' he puffed. 'Tell the
defence to seal the gaps.
Remind Kim about her volleys.'

Billy passed the instructions
on to the team.

'Billy's a good coach,' said Rick.

'Once he's warmed up,' added Joe.

The Tigers and the Gazelles faced each other across the centre line. Both teams had fast strikers. Both teams had strength in midfield and a solid defence. Both teams had their eye on the County Shield.

The referee blew his whistle for the match to start. The Gazelles kicked off. The crowd cheered. Play went swiftly from end to end. The Tigers could see that it was going to be a hard struggle. Every time they thought there was an opening, the Gazelles' defence were there.

Then at last there was a
chance. Bullseye tapped the ball
to Billy.

'To Ellen!' shouted Springer.

Billy could see Ellen running
down the wing. He punted the
ball into a space ahead of her.
She gathered it up, dodged

round the Gazelles' defence and
knocked it across to Bullseye.

'Take a shot!' shouted
Springer.

'Shoot, Bullseye!' yelled Billy.

Bullseye hammered the ball
into the back of the goal.

The Tigers were one-nil up.

They ran back to their positions.

'Well done, Tigers!' shouted Springer. 'That was a great goal. Now, tell Mona to watch out for the counter-attack. Get Terry to stick to that little striker. And tell Blocker . . . OUCH!'

'Tell Blocker ouch?' said Billy in surprise.

'I didn't do anything!' said Blocker crossly.

'Not you, Blocker,' sighed Billy.

He looked over to the touchline. Springer was rubbing his leg.

'What's going on?' called Billy.

'We're playing a football match,' giggled Ellen.

'It's all that loosening up,' laughed Terry. 'It's loosened up his brain!'

The whistle blew and the Gazelles kicked off. Springer got to his feet.

'Keep your eye on the game, Billy,' he called. 'The ball's

coming your way.'

Kim had possession. Billy ran to join her. Kim chipped the ball to Billy and ran forwards into the area. As the defenders came towards Billy, he tapped the ball to Kim again in a skilful one-two.

'Good play, Tigers!' yelled Springer. 'Watch out for that

number three. He's fast. And tell Kim to . . . GET OFF!'

'GET OFF!' repeated Billy before he could stop himself.

Kim was about to blast the ball at goal. She stopped, wobbled, and fell over.

'What do you mean – get off?' she shouted, as she sat on the pitch.

The Gazelles' goalie ran over and picked up the ball.

'Er . . . sorry, Kim,' muttered Billy. 'I . . . erm . . . I thought there was a dog behind me.'

The Gazelles' goalkeeper rolled the ball to one of his defenders. The defender kicked it up the field towards the Gazelles' attack.

'Tell Lisa to mark that striker,' yelled Springer. 'Get Rick to help her . . .'

'Lisa, mark that striker,' called Billy. 'Rick, help her.'

'. . . and LET GO OF MY SHORTS!' bellowed Springer.

'LET GO OF MY SHORTS!' repeated Billy.

'Never touched him!' shouted a large defender.

The referee blew his whistle and ran over.

'Sorry, ref,' mumbled Billy. 'Erm . . . It was that dog again . . . it attacked me.'

Everyone looked round for the dog.

'It's gone now,' said Billy quickly.

The Gazelles were giving Billy funny looks. The Tigers were giving Billy funny looks. Billy was getting desperate. What was wrong with Springer?

Billy couldn't stand it any more. He pretended he had cramp. He limped over to the

touchline. Springer was lying on his back.

'Springer!' whispered Billy anxiously. 'What's wrong?'

'I'll tell you what's wrong,' said a gruff voice.

Billy looked up. A man suddenly appeared in front of him. The man wore a football kit like Springer's, but it was dark and dirty. He was wobbly round the edges. And Billy could see right through him. It was like looking through a muddy puddle. The man was . . . a ghost. The ghost had small, beady eyes and short, bristly hair. He didn't look very friendly.

'I'm Smasher Smith,' snarled

the new ghost. 'Best striker and head-butter ever.'

Springer struggled to his feet.

'Smasher is a bit annoyed with me,' he puffed, rubbing his bruises. 'That penalty I saved when Tottingham Town won

the cup all those years ago –
that was *his* penalty.'

'It was the first penalty I ever
missed,' growled Smasher. 'And
I never got my own back. Now
I've tracked Springer down at
last. This is my chance for
revenge.'

'Leave him alone!' gasped
Billy. 'Springer is our coach.
We need him.'

'Coach, is he?' laughed
Smasher. 'We'll see what a
good coach he is – after I've
punched his lights out.'

He lunged at Springer.
Springer ducked and ran out
on to the pitch. Smasher ran
after him. Billy ran after
Smasher.

There was a sudden roar
from the Tigers' goal. Springer
stopped and looked round,

and Smasher took his chance. Smasher stood over Springer, rubbing his knuckles and grinning.

'Oh, Springer!' he sniggered.
'You've head-butted my fist!
You deserve a red card.'

'Get up, Springer!' whispered
Billy. 'We can't play without
you!'

'Stay there, Springer!' snarled
Smasher. 'The Tigers have a
new coach now – Smasher
Smith.'

Springer groaned and rubbed
his head.

'There can only be one
coach . . .' he said.

'That's right,' said Billy.

'. . . so I'm off,' mumbled
Springer. 'It's up to you, Billy.'

Springer was looking very
faint round the edges.

'Get rid of him . . . don't
forget . . . number seven . . .'

'Springer!' shouted Billy.
'Don't go!'

But Springer had faded away. Kim sprinted over to Billy.

'You're the one who'll have to go!' she shouted. 'While you've been messing about, the Gazelles have equalized.'

Billy walked slowly back to his position. Everything looked hopeless. Dad was still in the toilet. Springer had gone and Billy didn't know if he'd ever come back. And now they were stuck with a mad ghost as a coach! But Billy had no choice. He was a useless coach on his own. He'd have to give Smasher Smith a chance.

Bullseye kicked off to Billy. Billy dribbled feebly down the pitch and soon lost possession. Smasher ran alongside.

'Hack him down!' he snarled. 'Go for the man not the ball. Watch me!'

The ghost striker went in with both feet. It was a nasty tackle.

Well, it would have been a
nasty tackle if Smasher hadn't
been a ghost. He flew straight
through the Gazelles'
midfielder. The player didn't
notice a thing. She dribbled
round Billy.

'You can't do that!' said Billy
to Smasher.

'No, I can't,' said Smasher, crossly. 'But *you* can. And you should have. Look!'

Smasher pointed to the Tigers' goal. Billy turned just in time to see Mona dive and miss the ball by inches. The Gazelles were two-one up.

At half-time, the Tigers flopped down on the pitch and sucked at their oranges. They glared at Billy. Billy stared at his bootlaces.

'We won't be going home with the County Shield,' moaned Terry.

'I wish *I* could go home,' said Bullseye.

'How are we going to beat

the Gazelles?' said Mona.

'Head-butt them!' growled
Smasher.

'We can't head-butt them,'
muttered Billy.

'Course we can't!' said Joe, in
alarm.

'Kick their ankles!' snarled
Smasher.

'Kick their ankles?' said
Billy.

'We're a clean side, Billy!'
gasped Ellen.

What would Springer have
said now, thought Billy
desperately. If only he had
given some last-minute advice
before he disappeared. Then

Billy remembered Springer's words.

'I've got it!' he said, jumping up. 'Seven!'

'Seven what, Coach?' said Mona.

'It won't be goals,' moaned Rick.

'No,' said Billy. '*Number* seven.'

'I'm number seven,' said Rob. 'But I'm not doing any dirty tackles.'

'Not you, Rob,' sighed Billy.

'Who then?' asked Lisa.

'I dunno,' groaned Billy, as he paced up and down.

At that moment a pale figure, clutching a plastic bag,

appeared at the changing room door. It was Mr Bright.

'I'm okay now,' he called.

The Tigers leapt to their feet and cheered. Billy grinned. It was going to be all right. Dad was back. Then Mr Bright's face turned green. He clapped his hand over his mouth and disappeared again.

The referee blew his whistle and the second half began. Smasher Smith ran out gleefully on to the pitch.

'Right, Billy Bright,' he shouted. 'You need a bit of decent coaching.'

Billy had to get rid of this ghastly ghost. Springer had

tried to tell him how. It was
something to do with the
number seven. Billy put seven
Tigers in defence. It didn't
work. He put seven Tigers in
attack. That didn't work either.

He hopped on his left leg seven times. He hopped on his right leg seven times. But Smasher was still there, demonstrating how to wrong-foot the opposition.

'Smasher!' hissed Billy.

'Smash 'em?' gasped Joe. 'We can't do that.'

'There's something wrong with Billy,' muttered Terry.

'He'd better go off before he's sent off,' said Ellen.

Billy couldn't stand it any longer. The Tigers were going to lose the final – and it would look as if it was all his fault. If only he could explain. If only he could tell the team about Smasher.

He *could* tell the team about
Smasher! That's what Springer
meant! *Rule* number seven.
Only one person was supposed
to know about a ghost coach.
So, if he told the team about
Smasher, Smasher would
disappear!

'Listen everyone!' he yelled. Play stopped. The Tigers, the Gazelles and the crowd turned to gawp at Billy. Billy ran round the pitch, waving his arms and shouting.

Billy heard a roar of anger. Smasher was jumping up and down on the pitch, shaking his fists at Billy.

'You can't get rid of me, kid!' he yelled. 'I don't play by the rules. I'm staying.'

Smasher thrust his face right into Billy's.

'You'll be sorry you ever messed with Smasher Smith. You'll never win that shield!'

What could Billy do now? PhIFA rule number seven hadn't worked. Billy was stuck with Smasher – for ever. Then he realised that Smasher was shrinking.

Billy leapt in the air.

'Yippee!' he shouted.

'Billy's gone bonkers,' wailed Blocker.

'No I haven't,' said Billy,

looking round for Springer. 'I'm
all right now . . . *Springer!*'

There was no sign of the
ghost goalie.

'That dog must have bitten
Billy,' said Rob.

'No he didn't,' said Billy.
'*Springer!*'

'Must have been a mad dog,'
said Lisa.

'No it wasn't!' sighed Billy.

'What dog?' said Blocker, scratching his head.

The referee came over and pulled out a yellow card. He held it up to Billy and wrote his name in his book. It was a free kick to the Gazelles. The Tigers muttered angrily. Billy knew there was only one thing for it. He might be a useless coach, but he was a good striker. He had to show the team that they could still win.

The Gazelles' captain took the free kick. It was a long pass across the pitch. Billy sprinted forwards and intercepted the ball. He turned and set off towards the goal. He dodged one defender and wrong-footed

another and now there were
two more coming at him. He
looked round for support. But
no one had kept up with him. It
was up to Billy. He waited for
the defenders to reach him, then
he quickly tapped the ball
forwards and ran between

them. Billy knew he must shoot, and shoot quickly. And he did. The goalie didn't stand a chance. The crowd roared.

'Two-all,' yelled a voice from the top of the refreshment tent.

It was Springer! Springer slid down the roof of the tent, sailed over the heads of the crowd and landed next to Billy.

'Sorry I'm late getting back,' said Springer. 'I was looking for a plaster.'

It was only minutes before the end of the match. The Tigers needed one more goal.

'Come on, Tigers,' shouted Springer. 'You can do it!'

'Come on, Tigers,' shouted Billy. 'We can do it!'

The Gazelles kicked off and moved forwards with the ball.

'Tell Joe to tackle that striker,' called Springer. 'Tell Ellen and Rob to get up there in support.'

Joe faced the striker. As the striker went to pass the ball, he blocked it with his boot and

flicked it skilfully over to Terry.
Terry passed to Ellen, who
knocked the ball sideways to
Rob. Billy and Kim made a
forward run and Rob booted
the ball up the field to land
perfectly at Kim's feet. Kim
punted it to Bullseye but the
defenders moved in like wasps
round a jam jar. Bullseye
tapped the ball swiftly back to
Kim, who whacked it at goal.
The goalie did a tremendous
leap and punched the ball
away. The crowd gasped. Billy
ran forwards and dived. It was
a brilliant header. It was a
brilliant goal. Three-two to the
Tigers. The referee blew the
whistle for full time.

Billy and his team had done
it. The Tigers were the new
County Champions!

Other titles in the same series

Ghost Goalie
The Tigers football team are full of confidence about the next match. But their coach falls ill just before they are due to play! The Tigers are desperate. How can they win without him? Perhaps they can, with a very special bit of ghostly help . . .

Save the Pitch
It's the crucial last game of the season and the Tigers football team must win to go to the top of the League. But the pitch has been invaded by workmen laying new pipes, and it looks like the game will be called off. Can the Tigers get help – fast?

The Terrible Trainer
The Tigers football team have a substitute coach, but he is mean and shouts a lot. He makes the Tigers feel awful. How can they get rid of Mr Bawl and find a coach who will make sure they can win?

The Cup Final
The Tigers football team have to win this last game to win the Cup! But disaster strikes when their coach's head becomes stuck in some iron railings when trying to get the ball. What can they do to save the match?

Tigers on Television
The Tigers football team have a nail-biting match to play, and a local TV crew has come to film them in action. But the TV cameras have a terrible effect on the team's ghost trainer and he can't coach them properly! What can the Tigers do?

Ghost Striker